Skeleton in the Cupboard

Edna Taylor

Skeleton in the Cupboard

& other stories for young and old

Skeleton in the Cupboard & other stories for young and old
ISBN 978 1 74027 886 7
Copyright © text Edna Taylor 2014
Cover photo © paulmz – Fotolia.com

First published in this form 2014
Reprinted 2016

Ginninderra Press
PO Box 3461 Port Adelaide 5015
www.ginninderrapress.com.au

Contents

The Greenhouse Effect On Grandpa

It was a little house made of glass – just big enough to stand up in if you weren't too tall. Grandpa built it himself and, as he was a short person, anyone over five foot six had to be sure and keep their head ducked down or else they would knock into all the stuff hanging from the roof.

Grandpa spent a lot of time in his greenhouse and when we – my brother and I, that is – went to visit, the first thing we'd say to Grandma was, 'Where's Grandpa?' We always knew of course, but liked to watch Grandma's face as she rolled her eyes skywards and got a wry look on her face as she told us, 'Down in the greenhouse as usual.' Then we'd give her a quick hello kiss and scamper down the backyard, through the vegetable patch, jumping over the crazy paving that ran between half-dug potatoes and cabbages and carrots, then going very carefully until we came to the bottom of the garden where the greenhouse nestled under the big oak tree.

Our boisterous chatter stopped as we quietly opened and then closed the door behind us. We knew the penalties for banging the door, which Grandpa said disturbed the plants. He said they didn't like sudden noises.

It was always warm and clammy in the greenhouse even when it was cold outside. Lined up on the bench were the orchids and other beautiful plants I never remembered the names of, and tomatoes – big luscious tomatoes. They were the best, and whenever we came over for tea we always had salad from the garden and tomatoes from the greenhouse. It was quiet and peaceful and friendly in there. Here we would sit, my brother on a wooden crate and me on an old three-legged stool. 'Tell us about when you were a lad, Grandpa,' we'd say, and then he'd take his time rolling his baccy, which he kept in a little square tin, and stuffing it into the bowl of his pipe, sometimes using two or three matches to get it going.

Then when he was settled and puffing away, he'd get a faraway look in his eyes and tell us stories of his youth. How he ran away to be a sailor on a tramp steamer and sailed the seven seas, and the wondrous places he'd been to. We became lost in a world of adventure and wonder. Sometimes I think he made the stories up but we didn't mind. It was a magic time that was just between us and Grandpa.

He knew lots of stuff too. Once when I asked him why some of the greenhouse glass was painted white, he said that it reflected the sun's rays and stopped the greenhouse from getting too hot. He said that if everybody in the world painted the roof of their house white then the radiation could be controlled and it would stop the earth from getting too hot.

I told this to my teacher when she was explaining about the effects of too much carbon dioxide in the earth's atmosphere, and she looked at me a bit strangely. I think Grandpa was ahead of his time.

We'd hear Grandma calling out to us to come in for tea, and Grandpa would knock his pipe out and slowly stand, rubbing his back. 'Come on you two, we'd better go or your grandmother will start getting her wig off.'

I never really knew what that meant as I was sure Grandma didn't wear a wig. Then we'd go and join Mum and Dad and Grandma for tea.

Grandpa hardly ever spoke in the house. Grandma did all the talking. She never stopped. She was a natural talker, but it was all about what the neighbours were doing and what the butcher said and stuff like that. After a while, I used to stop listening.

The only times I heard Grandpa speak in the house was to say 'Thankee,' when someone passed him the salt or something. After tea, he'd just sit quietly in the corner and start rolling his baccy.

Once when we'd come back from the greenhouse, we were all

smiling and happy and Grandma looked at us suspiciously. 'You two have been gone a long time,' she said. 'I hope you haven't been bothering your grandfather. What have you been up to then? It all looks very suspicious to me.'

'It's the greenhouse effect,' said my brother, being smart, and I looked at Grandpa.

And he winked.

A Good Time

Gerry had got up to make a cup of tea from the motel's small bar. He had collected the morning paper from outside the door and now they lay comfortably in bed, he reading the financial pages and she reading the latest gossip.

'So where does your wife think you are this weekend?' the beautiful blonde asked.

'Oh, at a conference,' he said. 'Don't worry, she has no reason to suspect anything,'

'But when are you going to tell her about us?' she asked in a slightly whining voice. 'We can't go on like this. You have to tell her.'

'I will,' he said, giving her a cuddle. 'I promise. I just haven't found the right time.'

To himself he thought, the time is never going to be right. And anyway I quite like the way things are. Why rock the boat?

Later he lay in bed watching while she put on her make-up and polished her nails. She always went to such a lot of trouble to make herself look nice, he thought, as he dozed off.

After a lovely day spent mostly in bed, they had to rush to get dressed and get to the airport. They just made the flight back to Sydney.

Gerry arrived home quite late and crawled into bed beside his wife who barely stirred.

Next morning he awoke to a big thump on his shoulder and gasped. 'Ouch,' he cried. 'What are you doing?'

He looked angrily at his wife, who was staring intently at his feet where he had kicked the bedclothes off during the night.

'Do you have something to tell me?' she asked in a strange voice.

He looked down and was speechless with horror when he saw the bright purple nail polish on each big toe.

He couldn't speak. His wife glared at him. 'When you're ready to talk…' she said. 'Right now would be a good time.'

Lucky Socks

Emily volunteered at the Salvation Army shop. It gave her something to do. Stopped her from feeling useless with no purpose in life after Tom had passed away.

She happened to be there when someone brought in yet another box of old clothes to be sorted out. It was surprising the things people brought in sometimes, she thought. Stuff that, quite frankly, was so old and useless that it would have to go straight into the rubbish bin.

Emily started sorting the contents into piles of good to sell and no good to sell. There were neatly folded old-fashioned suits, shirts and jumpers. Most of it was in very good condition and, judging from the style, obviously from an older gentleman's wardrobe.

In the bottom of the box, underneath everything else, was a rolled-up pair of socks. Nobody buys used socks, thought Emily. She picked them up and unrolled them. Brown woollen, and obviously hand-knitted, with a lovely neat darn over one heel. There was a tape with something written on it sewn inside the back of one of the socks, and Emily peered closely to see what it said.

She froze for a second or two, then she felt herself going wobbly and had to sit down quickly.

'Are you OK, Em?' Marg was coming over looking concerned.

'Yes, I'm fine. It's just…well, this is so strange.' She held out the sock. 'Look, see.' She smoothed out the tape with writing on it. 'This is my name, or at least it was before I married Tom.'

There, embroidered neatly, was 'Socks knitted by Emily Green'.

She cast her mind back to the days of the Second World War in England, when all the girls in her class at school were taught to knit. They knitted socks for the army, which were collected up by the Red

Cross and sent over to where the soldiers were fighting. The girls never knew who received their socks but were encouraged to put their names inside if they wanted. So Emily did. She had recently learnt to embroider and she was pleased with her handiwork. She had carefully sewed the tape inside the sock and hoped that whoever received them appreciated them, and that they fitted.

'It's been over sixty years,' she said now, in awe. 'All that time ago. I can't believe it. Marg, do you know the lady who brought this box of clothes in?'

Suddenly she knew she had to find out more. A little sliver of excitement shot through her body as she contemplated the absolutely incredible chance of finding a pair of socks she had actually knitted all that time ago, landing up here in Australia.

'Yes,' said Marg, sounding almost as excited as Emily. 'She lives locally. She often brings in donations. I think her name is Jordan. Yes, that's it. Jess Jordan. I think we have her address in the register. Sometimes people like feedback, or we contact them if we're looking for something specific that they might be able to get.'

She bustled off, leaving Emily still looking reverently at the socks, then came back with the phone number. 'There you go. Are you going to phone them up, then?'

'Yes,' said Emily, now feeling calmer. 'I have to find out how this has happened.' She couldn't wait to get home and make the call.

Jess Jordan sounded friendly, interested and intrigued. She invited Emily to call around the next day for a coffee. And to bring the socks. She said she had a story to tell about the socks which Emily would enjoy.

Next day, Emily drove to Jess Jordan's house in a state of mild excitement. Jess was a lady in her fifties, friendly, like her voice on the phone.

Emily produced the socks from her bag, which she placed on the table alongside the coffee cups.

Jess picked them up and looked inside the top. 'Yes,' she said, 'that's them. Thank goodness. I thought I'd lost them. They must have rolled into that box of clothes when I was packing it up.' She smiled at Emily, 'They're my dad's.'

'Your dad's?' Suddenly Emily felt bereft. 'That box of clothes you brought in to the Salvos, were they his? Has he…has he…passed away, then?'

'Oh no, he's well.' Jess smiled. 'He's been on his own since Mum died about ten years ago, and now he's finally sold his house. He didn't want those old clothes any more so I packed them up for the Salvos. But he got upset when he realised he couldn't find his socks. These are very special, you see.'

Emily was hanging on to every word. 'Special socks?' she asked.

'Yes, Emily. These were his lucky socks. They went with him through the war and after the war. Around the world. He wouldn't part with them. He didn't wear them so much after the war, but he always kept them. I remember a big argument once with Mum when she tried to throw them out. He always said they brought him luck, and he always wished he could have thanked the lass who knitted them.'

Emily was quite overcome. 'Oh, my goodness,' she said. 'I always wondered who'd got them.'

Jess grinned a bit mischievously 'Well then, how would you like to meet him?'

Emily was stuck for words. 'Do you think he'd mind?' she finally said. 'I think I would really like that.'

Jess handed her the socks. 'You could take these with you.'

And so she did. Jess took her to the retirement village where she introduced Emily to her dad Bob, and then quietly left, saying she had things to do and would pick Emily up in a couple of hours.

Warm brown eyes in a weatherbeaten face gazed steadily at Emily as he grasped her hand. 'Hello, Emily,' he said. 'Jess told me about you. Over the years I often wondered. My lucky socks never let me down. Every time we went into battle, I wore them. And here you are. Living proof. Who would've thought…'

He was looking at her as though she was a miracle, which indeed, thought Emily, it surely feels like it is.

She brought the socks out from her bag and passed them over to Bob. 'And here are your socks. I hope your good luck continues,' she added with a bit of a shy smile.

'Oh, I've got a feeling it will.' Bob was smiling at her.

And Emily thought that perhaps she wouldn't be spending so much time at the Salvos in future.

Brassed Off

Sally liked to go to the markets on the weekends. She would browse around the second-hand stalls, and prided herself on being able to spot a bargain.

One day she found an old lamp, badly tarnished, and thought that with a little bit of cleaning up it would look quite good. It looked like the sort of lamp in which you would have to put oil or paraffin. It would also need a new wick. But she liked antiques and, as it was only five dollars, she bought it.

Sally couldn't wait to get home and clean up the lamp and see what it was made of. She thought it was brass and looked in the cupboard for the Brasso. But it had been so long since she had used it for anything that it had all dried up and was useless. Muttering to herself, she chucked the bottle into the bin and looked at the clock. It was too late to go to the supermarket. Her cleaning job would have to wait till tomorrow.

Sally had another look at the lamp and wondered where it had come from. She shook it gently and thought she could hear a small thump of something moving inside. Intrigued and curious now, she decided that tomorrow she would take the lamp to bits.

Next day at the supermarket, Sally bought some cleaning stuff, hurried home and proceeded to attack the lamp with gusto. A lovely shine was appearing with a beautiful pattern emerging all around the sides.

She prised open the middle bit where the oil container had been inserted and finally got it out. Holding the lamp upside down, she gave it a shake. Sally couldn't wait to find out what was in the bottom, and out fell a little piece of rolled-up paper. Gently she unrolled it to find a tiny scroll with writing on it. Not that her knowledge of languages was great, but she thought it seemed to be in Arabic.

Feeling quite excited now, Sally put it to one side and finished cleaning the lamp, which was now looking quite beautiful, and then thought about how to decipher the writing on the little scroll.

She didn't know anyone who could help. So she decided to phone the librarian at the local library, who suggested Sally bring the paper in and have a look at the language books to try and get a clue. So off she went to the library, and found a dictionary in Arabic/English. Yes, she thought, it looks similar. That was a good guess. So Sally borrowed the book and went home determined to get to the bottom of the mystery.

Next day, she laboriously copied out the symbols as best as she could from something written so small, and then started at the beginning of the dictionary trying to find something that matched. There was nothing. No way could she find anything exactly resembling the symbols.

Feeling rather frustrated, Sally finally had a brainwave and rang up the museum and told her story to a kind-sounding lady. To her delight, she suggested Sally bring the whole lot – lamp and scroll – into the foreign artefacts department and they would have a go at translation.

Next day, it was a train to the city and a walk along to the museum, where after much wandering around Sally finally found the lady she had talked to on the phone.

'Let's have a look,' she said, and gently took the lamp out of the tissue paper in which Sally had carefully wrapped it. Getting out a little magnifying glass, she scrutinised the writing on the scroll. She shook her head then, picking up the phone, dialled a number and asked someone if they could call in to her office for a moment. A few minutes later, a dark-skinned gentleman arrived and together they studied the writing.

'Where did you get this?' he asked with a curious smile on his face.

'At the market,' said Sally. 'I thought it looked like an interesting antique.'

'It is indeed,' he said, 'a very nice lamp. Unfortunately, this type is pretty common. Not really an antique, I'm afraid.'

Sally was a bit deflated but pressed on. 'But what does the writing say?' she asked him. 'Can you read it?'

'Oh yes,' he said. 'It says "Made in China", written in very bad Arabic.'

Mrs Billings

The old lady used to sit on the park bench by the lake feeding the ducks. Everyday she'd be there, like part of the landscape, dressed in black, with a skirt that seemed to be almost green with age. She wore lace-up boots with pointy toes and an old felt hat pulled down over wispy grey hair. She kept a walking stick by her side which she would grasp at nervously if anyone came too close to her bench.

I went to the park most days to eat the sandwiches the hostel handed out. I never saw the old lady arrive and I never saw her leave, but I couldn't help noticing that nobody ever stopped to chat or pass the time of day with her. I thought she must be as lonely as I was. She reminded me of my grandma in a way, and I think that's why I suddenly decided one day to take a chance and sit down beside her on her bench to eat my lunch, instead of sprawling out on the grass as I usually did.

I opened my sandwiches, wondering if I should say something. I could sense the slight drawing away of her body and the quick turn of her head as she glanced at me, and then away again.

She grabbed hold of her walking stick and for a moment I thought she was going to hit me with it.

'Nice day,' I said.

She turned to look at me, and a worried pair of old eyes surrounded by a face wrinkled like a walnut gazed at me with apprehension. Her bag of food scraps dropped to the ground.

Quickly, I bent to pick it up and handed it to her.

She hesitated a moment, then, 'Thank you, young man,' she said quietly.

Well, that's broken the ice a bit, I thought, and tried again. 'I've seen you here before,' I remarked. 'Do you come here every day to feed the ducks?'

But she ignored me, so I kept quiet and ate my lunch, watching her throw bits of bread into the water.

'Maybe I'll see you tomorrow,' I said, as I stood to leave.

'Maybe,' she replied shortly, without turning her head, 'and maybe not.'

Next day, though, there she was in her usual place, so I sat down beside her again. She didn't acknowledge my presence for a while. I might as well have been invisible.

Then, suddenly she asked, 'Well, young man, what's your name?'

I was so surprised I nearly choked on my sandwich. 'Jack Potter. What's yours?'

'None of your business!'

'I told you my name, didn't I?' I responded, a bit cheeky like.

She hesitated a moment. 'Mrs Billings,' she said.

'Well, I'm pleased to meet you, Mrs Billings,' I replied.

She relaxed a bit then and I offered her a sandwich, but she shook her head. I didn't have much time that day. I had finally got a job interview lined up, so I left soon after, without any conversation except to say goodbye.

But then she said, 'Goodbye, Jack,' and I caught a bit of a twinkle in her eyes, as though she had decided I was weird but probably harmless.

The next day she wasn't there. I looked around the park and the lake. The old lady was probably sick of seeing me hanging around. All the same, I had this feeling that something bad had happened, like when my grandma had suddenly had her heart attack, and I had known. Even though I wasn't there when it happened, I'd just known.

I found one of the gardeners who worked around the park. 'Do you know the old lady who sits on the bench over there?' I asked him.

He nodded. 'Yeah, I've seen her. Don't know who she is, though. Comes here every day regular as clockwork. Funny old girl,' he added.

'Her name is Mrs Billings,' I told him. 'Do you know where she lives?'

Nope.' He thought a minute. 'I've seen her going that way out of the park, though.' He pointed towards the bridge over the main road. Then he leaned forward. 'She was mugged once, you know. Young bloke about your age. Snatched her bag. Knocked her off the bench.'

He was starting to eye me suspiciously, so I told him thanks and quickly left. I started walking in the direction he had indicated.

Over the bridge, there were big posh houses. No way, I thought. No way would she live around here. She probably comes on the bus.

I was about to head back when I saw those black pointy-toed shoes sticking out from behind the base of the big brick mail box at the gate of the next house. Heart thumping, I ran forward and there she was. Lying in a heap, with her bag beside her spilling bits of food onto the driveway.

She was alive and sort of gasping for breath. I looked around but there was no one in sight. Luckily there was a phone box nearby, so I rang emergency services and the ambulance got there pretty quick. I went with her to the hospital and hung around till they said she'd be okay.

I went to visit Mrs Billings the next day with some flowers I had got from the park and she seemed really happy to see me. She said I'd restored her faith in human nature, and other embarrassing stuff like that.

That's all really. That's how come I'm living in this big house. Mrs Billings found out I was living at the hostel and when she came home from the hospital she offered me a room. We get along just great. I sorta pretend she's my grandma and keep an eye on things around the house.

Mrs B doesn't go to the park to feed the ducks so much these days. She says she's got enough to do feeding me. But she looks happy all the time now instead of sad and lonely like she used to.

And that's what it's all about really, isn't it?

The Lottery Ticket

'Call a doctor!' George exclaimed excitedly. 'I think I'm going to have a heart attack!'

'What are you shouting about?' Millie popped her head around the kitchen door 'It sounded like you said you were having a heart attack.'

'I did. No. Not really. I mean, I'm not actually having a heart attack!' He could scarcely contain himself. 'Look!' He held up the notepad as she came towards him. 'We've got five numbers. Hush a minute.' He waved his pen as Millie started to speak. 'Here comes the last one.'

'Number 11,' the man calling the numbers said, 'and good luck to you all.'

'Well?' Millie grabbed the pad from George's hand. 'How many did we get, then?' She tried to keep the excitement out of her voice.

Never had they won. Not once. Not even the fifth dividend. They'd always had the same numbers. She knew them by heart. Hers and George's birthdays, their two children's birthdays and the grandchildren's birthdays. George often said that they should change numbers but she never would. 'One day they'll come up,' she would say. 'One day, just you wait and see.'

Millie tried to still the beating of her heart which seemed to be taking over the whole of her body. Already she was mentally buying new carpets, picturing a leather lounge suite and a new kitchen. Holidays in Europe, money for the children.

Shakily she looked at the numbers, then slowly gave the notepad to George and collapsed onto the lounge chair. 'Oh, my goodness,' she whispered, 'you're right. They all match. All six. Oh, George.' And then, because she was so overcome, Millie started to cry.

George's mind was also busy. But he wasn't thinking about carpets and holidays. He looked across at his wife. Typical, he thought. We have a win and she has to cry.

He looked at the short plump lady with greying hair and the lines of wear on her face, now blotchy and unattractive, and his mind's eye quickly filled with the vision of Amanda. The beautiful Amanda who worked in reception at his office. He thought about her long perfect legs and her golden hair, and the way she always had that special smile for him. The way she stood close enough for him to smell her perfume.

George was fifty and he considered himself to be in the prime of his life. All he lacked was enough money to make that final break and make a fresh start with someone like Amanda. Amanda liked nice things. With a figure like hers, George thought, she deserved the best. And now he could make it happen.

'Stop that snivelling,' he said to Millie. 'What on earth are you crying about?'

'Because I'm so happy.' She scrunched up her hanky and shoved it into her apron pocket. 'I'll have to phone and tell the children.'

George got up quickly and held out his hand. 'Well, let me have the ticket, then. I'll check with the lottery office and find out what we have to do.'

Millie looked at him. Her voice came out a little wavery. 'But you've got it, George. Don't you remember? I asked you to pick it up because I didn't have time to go to the mall this week.' She trailed off as she saw the look of complete disbelief on his face.

'You stupid woman.' he shouted. 'I told you I wasn't going that way and you said you'd get it in the morning. Are you telling me you didn't get it?' He was beside himself with fury. 'You always were stupid,' he raged. 'You couldn't even do a simple thing like pick up a lottery ticket. Every week we've had one for twelve years. A normal person wouldn't forget something they've been doing for twelve years, would they? And now look what's happened. The numbers finally came up…and…aah…' George was clutching his chest as he collapsed onto the floor.

The funeral was over, and Millie's daughter Jane had been helping to clean up in the wake of friends and neighbours who had stayed around to chat about George. They said how lucky it was that he hadn't had to suffer, although of course fifty was quite young to go these days, wasn't it? And how strange to have a heart attack like that, out of the blue. And the sad shaking of heads. 'You never know when your time has come,' they said. 'Poor Millie, it's such a tragedy.'

When everyone had gone, Millie and Jane finally sat down for a cup of tea, and suddenly Jane delved into her handbag.

'By the way, Mum,' she said, 'what with poor Dad and everything that's happened, I forgot to give you your lottery ticket. You remember you asked me to get it for you? Well – there you go. I picked out all the usual numbers.' She put the ticket down on the table. 'I don't suppose you got around to checking it yet, did you. What with Dad's funeral and everything.'

She leaned forward and looked closely at her mother, who had gone strangely quiet.

A smile spread slowly across Millie's face as she reached into her pocket for her hanky.

'Mum?' Jane looked puzzled. 'What are you looking so happy about?'

Slash and Burn

Percy Potter looked up at the sky. Nice and clear. The weather forecast was for rain at the weekend, so today he had better get on with it.

He could hear in his head the voice of Duggie, his old mate – a retired major in the British army who had never lost his plummy accent and all things British. 'You've gotta bite the bullet, old chap.' Duggie had been through it and knew what he was talking about. 'Slash and burn,' he'd said. 'That's the only way to do it. Slash and burn.'

Percy looked at the boxes lining the walls of the garage. His life was in those boxes. His and Dora's. And although he knew what had to be done eventually, he had put it off as long as possible. Now the house was being sold and he had to clear everything out. He couldn't take it with him.

Percy let out a huge sigh and started dragging the boxes off the bench. They were heavier than they used to be, he thought. But then he had not lifted any of them for a long time, some not for years. He realised that his muscles just weren't so strong any more. He felt anger at the frailty of old age. The inevitability of it all.

Percy gave himself a mental shake. Just get on with it, old man, he thought. So he dropped the boxes on to the floor and dragged them outside, down the path and over to the old forty-gallon drum he used for burning garden rubbish. He couldn't lift the boxes up high enough to tip everything out so he began taking out the contents. Receipts, bills, letters he'd kept ever since he'd lived in the house, thirty years' worth. He had always kept it all. It was part of his life. He had never been able to throw anything away.

'Just in case, you never know when you might need it,' he'd tell Dora, his wife. But it had never been needed. It had all sat on the garage bench and every now and again, when there was no room left on the shelf inside the house, he would add a new box. Everything was carefully sorted and dated.

Mentally biting the bullet, Percy started chucking everything into the drum. He had a match ready and dropped it on top of the first batch, where it soon caught. In the next box were copies of all the letters he'd written, to the council, to the tax office, the newspapers. Percy had been a prolific letter writer, and now they all went into the fire. Then there were the old power bills, the gas, the phone, insurances long past their final dates, warranties all long-expired. Then the magazines, the old *Readers Digest* books. He thought briefly about adding them to the Salvos box but threw them in the fire anyway. Gradually the boxes emptied. He squashed them down and put them in the recycle bin.

Then it was done. Percy was tired now and sat down on the garden seat. He was lost in thought for a bit. His past life had just gone up in smoke. He was feeling a bit bereft, a bit sad, but strangely proud of himself. He never thought he would have been able to do it, but he had. And then it slowly dawned on him that it really didn't matter quite as much as he thought it would.

He watched as his daughter's car drew up at the front gate.

She saw him and called out, 'Are you ready to go, Dad?' She got out of the car and picked up two suitcases waiting by the front gate.

Jess was about to take him to the retirement home, where Duggie was already settled in. She glanced at the smoke still curling away from the old drum and then at Percy.

'Are you all right, Dad?'

'I'm good, love.'

He got into the car and looked back over the gate for a long moment. Then he firmly faced the front. 'Let's go,' he said.

Nearly Dead and Dateless

Mary turned on her headlights as the evening darkened. She had left the town behind and was on an unlit country road. She was on her way to a blind date, something that she had never done before and was totally out of character.

Bob was his name, and she had met him on an internet dating service which her friend Betty had dared her to go on. But he had a warm friendly voice on the phone and when he had finally called and asked her out, Mary had not taken too long to say OK. She was thinking about this, wondering if she was doing the right thing. She had never been to the restaurant where they had decided to meet for the first time, and was hoping she would be able to find it.

Her musings were rudely interrupted when suddenly she realised that the car in front had suddenly started waving about the road. It looked as though the driver had lost control. Mary braked, ready to stop, when the other car suddenly veered off the road, glanced off a tree and careered down the embankment on the side of the road.

Her heart thumping, Mary drove closer and stopped where the car had disappeared. She fumbled for her phone in her bag and ran to the edge. She could only just see the car in the dark. It seemed to have landed on its side. Frantically she looked along the road. Not one other car was in sight. This was not a widely used road; it was away from the main highway and a shortcut to the town where she was headed.

Mary quickly dialled triple O. The operator asked which service she required.

'I need an ambulance,' she said, feeling a bit panicky. 'A car has had an accident. It's gone over the side of the road.'

'Where are you?' asked the operator.

Mary told her the name of the road. She repeated her name and address twice.

'Why do you need to know this?' she asked. 'You need to get the ambulance here, and probably the police,' she added. 'The driver may have been drunk. I don't even know if he is still alive,' she said.

'Don't worry, dear,' said the calm voice on the other end of the phone. 'The ambulance is on its way. Now will you stay there until the police arrive? They'll need to take a statement.'

'But I can't. I'm on my way to an appointment. I'll be late.' Even as she said it, Mary knew that she wouldn't be going, not now. She would have to wait.

She looked down towards the crashed car. She looked along the road. Not a sound, nothing in sight. She would have to see if there was anything she could do. Carefully she stepped over the broken fence and slowly made her way down the embankment. It was muddy from recent rain but it wasn't as steep as it had seemed at first glance.

There was not a sound as she gingerly made her way down to the wreck. It was lying on its side, and the driver seemed to be attached by his seat belt, awkwardly squashed against the door. The window was smashed and an arm was dangling outside. His head had a lot of blood on it and his eyes were shut.

Oh my god, she whispered, I think he's dead. He looked quite lifeless lying there and she felt overwhelmed. Mary had never been so close to a car crash victim. Gingerly she took hold of his arm and felt for a pulse. She could feel nothing. Maybe I'm not doing it right, she thought. Maybe he's just unconscious.

'It's OK,' she said. 'Just you hang in there. The ambulance is coming. My name is Mary.'

Bravely she carried on chatting, trying to think of something to say just in case he could hear, even if he couldn't respond. She had read somewhere that sometimes people who appeared to be unconscious could still hear even if they couldn't move. So she continued.

'I'll stay with you until the ambulance arrives. So don't give up, OK? You're going to be all right.'

She stopped and listened. Thank goodness, she thought. At last. She could hear the ambulance. Quickly she scrambled back up to the road and stood there waving her arms.

It was another half hour or more before the police had been and taken her statement, and the ambos had finally freed the man and loaded him into the ambulance. She was still busy talking to the policeman when they left for the hospital, so she still didn't know whether he was alive or dead.

She looked at her watch. She would have been nearly an hour and a half late for her date. There was no way Bob was going to still be there. She realised she had left his phone number on the pad by the phone and couldn't ring him. She looked down at her mud-encrusted shoes and the bottoms of her best pants. Tired, she drove home and rang the mobile number of her now dateless date. There was no answer, so she left a text message, saying she would call again tomorrow.

Next day there was no answer, or reply, so Mary got on line again, and sent an email explaining what had happened to delay her the previous evening. Again there was no reply. He probably thought I'd got cold feet and stood him up, she thought sadly. Oh well, that's it then, I suppose.

The rest of the week passed in its usual way, work, shopping, housework. Mary occasionally wondered how the accident victim had got on, whether in fact he was still alive.

When the telephone rang one evening, she wasn't prepared for the sound of Bob's voice.

'Hi, Mary,' he said. 'It's me, Bob.'

'Oh, Bob,' she said, feeling awkward. 'I'm fine, how are you? I sent you an email. I'm sorry about our date.'

'Yes,' he said, 'I've only just read it, that's why I rang. To let you know.'

'Let me know?' asked Mary.

'That I've been in hospital,' he said. 'I was in an accident. My car crashed when I tried to avoid hitting a roo. I was on my way to a date.'

Mary couldn't say anything; everything was suddenly too weird.

'Was that you?' she managed at last.

'Yes, Mary,' he said, 'and it was you, wasn't it? You came and stayed with me. You talked to me. You called the ambos. You saved my life. I had a broken arm and was concussed, but I could hear you. I thought I was dreaming. I've just found out from the police who it was called the ambulance.'

Mary could barely speak. 'I thought you were dead,' she said, 'I didn't know what had happened. I didn't know what to do. Oh, I'm so glad you're OK.' She suddenly felt so happy, she didn't know what else to say.

'So what about our date, then?' Bob asked. 'Is it still on?'

Bobby's Luck

For weeks now, Bobby Johnson had been trying to get a date with Susie who worked at the deli. He used any excuse be could think of as a reason for his many visits to the shop.

Today he was making headway. There were no other customers, and he had decided to get a lottery ticket and was taking his time, chatting about the various combinations of numbers to choose from, when Susie suddenly pointed over his shoulder towards the window.

'Is that your car?' she asked. 'It seems to be moving.'

Bobby turned and, sure enough, his pride and joy, the green Holden he had spent many painstaking hours restoring, was slowly rolling away from the curb.

Oh no, he thought, it couldn't happen again. He rushed to the door and watched in horror as the car moved slowly forward, gathering speed as it started down the hill. There were no cars parked in front of it to stop the progress and Bobby could barely believe his eyes. He had only just finished knocking out the dents and patching up the paint.

His legs were pumping hard as he tried to catch up with it. 'Stop. Stop that car,' he yelled.

But no one took any notice. In fact, probably no one realised that it was driverless.

The Holden gathered speed as it progressed down the hill toward the traffic lights at the bottom.

'Please don't let there be a red light,' he thought in panic.

By a miracle, the lights changed to green and cars coming from either side stopped as the old Holden sailed past the intersection with Bobby not too far behind.

Unfortunately, the car was veering to the left as it travelled. It mounted the pavement and came to rest with a gentle crunch against a stobie pole.

A similar thing had happened last week. Luckily the car had been parked in the driveway that time and Bobby had managed to jump in and stop it, but not before it backed into the gate post, smashing the rear light.

He knew the brakes weren't a hundred per cent, but he always remembered to leave it in gear and park it with the wheels turned towards the kerb to stop it rolling. In fact, he intended taking it to the garage after leaving the deli today to sort out the brakes. But he had been so busy thinking about Susie he had been careless, again.

Puffing and panting, he finally reached his car, passing in front of the cars stopped at the lights, and heard an excited boy shout at his father, 'Look, Dad, a remote-controlled car,'

'Don't think so, son,' was the reply. 'I think that chap's chasing it.'

Bobby looked with sad resignation at the new, rather large dent and scrape on the passenger side door.

Jack Black the local policeman who, unfortunately for Bobby, had been sitting at the lights, did a double take when he realised there was no one in the driver's seat as the old Holden went past. His wheels made a satisfactory squeal as he sped around the corner to find out who the idiot was.

Bobby sighed as the police car drew up behind him and he turned to face the policeman.

'OK,' said Jack, holding out his hand 'Let's see your licence, then.'

Bobby dug it out of his wallet.

Jack took a long time looking at it and then, getting out his book, started writing down all the particulars. 'You realise you could have killed somebody.'

Bobby decided to play it cool and try to make light of the whole situation. 'Sorry, officer,' he grinned. 'It kind of got away from me. It won't happen again.'

'You bet it won't.'

'Well, nobody got hurt, did they?'

But the policeman wasn't listening. He walked around the car, kicking the tyres. 'You realise your tires have got no tread?'

'Er, yes, I was on my way to the garage to get new ones.'

'What about the brakes?'

'Well, I'm getting them fixed as well.'

'You realise you can't drive this car in its present state?'

'Well, I was just going to the garage, wasn't I?'

'You'll have to get it towed.'

Thus it was that Bobby had no wheels for a couple of weeks. His pride and joy was in the garage car yard, while he tried to get enough money together to pay for everything.

His dad had given him the car to use just to get him to work and back. It had been sitting in the shed for years, and Bobby was very proud of the progress he had been making on the restoration, even if it was taking more money and time that he had anticipated.

So now there would be a fine, and maybe a court appearance. It was all very depressing, and he didn't get to the deli again for a week. For one thing, he had to walk everywhere and get a bus to work and he had no car to take Susie out, even if he could get up the courage to ask her.

So when eventually he got to the deli after the twenty-minute walk from home, Bobby was unprepared for the big smile Susie gave him.

'Thank goodness,' she said. 'Here you are.'

Bobby looked around. The shop was empty, so she must have been talking to him.

'Hello, Susie,' he said. 'Yes, it's me. Here I am.' He looked a little bemused.

'I didn't know where you lived,' Susie said now, 'so I haven't been able to tell you. I was hoping you'd call in. I was worried,' she added, 'in case you were sick or had moved away or something.'

Bobby was feeling happier by the minute. She had actually missed him, he thought.

'Well, I had a bit of a problem,' he started to explain, 'with my car. It…um…ran down the hill, and there was a copper…'

Susie was flapping her hands to hush him up. 'But you see,' she said, 'when you left that day, you didn't come back for your lottery ticket. So I kept it for you,' she paused dramatically, 'and it won!'

'It won?' Bobby was feeling very happy now. 'I won?' he repeated. She nodded.

'Well, thanks heaps, Susie. Um…did I like…win much?'

'$50,000.'

He gasped. '$50.000?'

'Yes, and you have to go to the lottery office to collect it.' She reached under the counter, produced the ticket with a flourish and handed it to him. 'There you go.'

Then to a delighted Bobby she added, 'You'd probably have enough now to buy a new car, wouldn't you?'

She was leaning over the counter capturing him with bright brown eyes and, Bobby thought, looking more interested in him then she'd ever been before.

Bobby thought about the old bomb waiting for him in the yard which had suddenly stopped being his pride and joy. It was an accident waiting to happen. He couldn't take the risk. He couldn't let it happen again. One day he'd fix it up properly.

In the meanwhile… He cast adoring eyes at Susie and asked the question, 'What's your favourite colour, then?'

The Once a Year Day

Joe Selby sat at the table polishing his war medals. His fingers were stiff with arthritis and they grasped the cloth awkwardly as he worked.

Then he stood up slowly, rubbing the small of his back as he crossed the room and reached into a cupboard, removing a pair of well-worn leather boots. These he carried back to the table and set them down onto a sheet of newspaper.

Joe began polishing the boots, spitting onto the leather to improve the shine. He was too engrossed to hear the door open quietly behind him, but he knew his wife was there, and his hand stopped moving. He didn't turn round, but quietly waited for the words he knew would come.

'I suppose you think you're going on the march again this year.'

Her voice sounded angry. It always did. It was the way it came out, but Joe knew that the concern was there too, even though she never showed it.

'Well?' She came around the table, old eyes glaring accusingly at him.

He looked up at her, then started his polishing again. 'Yes,' he said.

Joe was stubborn. Every year since she could remember he had gone on the march, but the past few years he had come home exhausted.

Always she told him the same. 'That's the last time you're going, you foolish old man. What are you trying to do, kill yourself?'

But he would never answer, never admit he was getting too old.

'Well, you won't be going if it rains, will you?' she asked now. 'The weather forecast is for rain.'

'It won't be raining,' he said.

Next morning was cloudy, but dry, and Joe dressed with care while his wife silently cooked breakfast. Afterwards she stood at the doorway and watched as he walked slowly up the street to the bus stop.

By the time he had reached the city, Joe could feel his heart beating faster with anticipation, and felt the stirring excitement within himself as he heard the sound of the brass bands playing.

He turned round as a familiar voice hailed him and the wrinkles on his face merged in a chuckle of delight as he grasped his old mate's hand.

'Hiya, Charlie,' he shouted. 'How ya going?'

'Great Joe, just great. You're looking good, old son. How's the missus?'

Then there were other handshakes and slaps on the back. The joyous recognition of friends from the past and relief to see them still here, and the sorrow at the news of an old mate passing on.

'Did you hear about Tom, then?

'Yeah – a coupla months back. Heart attack. Still, you're looking great, mate...'

And so it went, until they were lining up for the march and waiting for their turn to start.

Then they were away, marching proudly with everyone in step. Somehow, Joe's back had stopped aching and his feet were keeping in time with the band. His legs were swinging along as though they didn't belong to him. He looked down at his medals glowing in the sunshine which had emerged from behind the cloud.

Glancing sideways at Charlie, Joe felt the same comradeship he'd felt all those years ago when they'd been holed up in the trenches waiting for the shells to burst around them. He smiled at the crowds of people lining the pavement along the roadside and listened to the band up the front playing all the old songs that he only ever heard on ANZAC days.

Joe knew that he would soon be getting tired and that if he stopped marching he'd never get started again, but it was as though his spirit and the joy of the day were stronger than his physical weakness. It seemed as though he had spent the whole year gathering strength to be used on his once a year day. As always, it had all been worth the waiting.

Later on, standing in front of the Cross of Sacrifice with his head bowed, Joe remembered and gave thanks for his life that was spared, and asked for the strength to carry through to next year.

He only had one drink at the pub afterwards before catching the bus back home again. He knew his limits and was dog-tired, but the glow and the glory of the day stayed with him as he slowly made his way along the street to his house. Deep down, he knew he had probably gone on the march for the last time, but he wasn't ready to admit defeat yet.

Joe straightened his shoulders and braced himself for the usual greeting from his wife who was waiting in the doorway.

'Look at you,' she started. 'That's the last time...' Then she stopped and peered closely at him. All she saw was the light of resolve in his eyes and the satisfied expression of a day well spent. She knew when she was beaten so she held her tongue and with a sigh of resignation led him inside. 'I suppose you'd like a cup of tea, then?'

Joe nodded and smiled, and carefully replaced his medals in the old tin box.

To Market To Market

It was your basic piggy bank. A pink one that Lucy had bought at the market for two dollars. It was one of those that couldn't be opened unless you smashed it. She turned it over slowly, giving it a little shake. Something rattled. So Lucy found a knife that just fitted into the opening and turned the piggy bank upside down in an effort to see what was inside. But the slot wasn't big enough for the knife and the coin to slide out. So she put the piggy bank next to the phone box, where every now and again someone would put a coin in. Mostly it was Lucy, and the box grew slowly but steadily heavier.

She forgot about the original coin that was in it and some time later, when the money box was fairly full, she was holding it thoughtfully, when her daughter Sally came in.

'How much do you reckon is in there, Mum?' she asked,

Lucy deliberated. 'Dunno, love, but I think I'll keep it for a while, for a rainy day.'

She put the box into the sideboard drawer under the tablecloths, and the next time she went shopping picked up another money box from the bank. One that you could open from the bottom.

Everyone forgot about the piggy bank except for Lucy. Sometimes when things were looking particularly bad and money was needed for the light or phone bills, or one of the children needed new shoes or school equipment, she remembered the piggy bank and was tempted to break it open. But no, she thought, we can manage.

And so they did. Even when Lucy's husband decided he wanted a younger woman, and left one day with a girl from his office, taking half the house hold goods with him, she managed.

Then one day Lucy realised that now the children were taking care of themselves, she had at last time to herself. She could do as she pleased, and the prospect was more exciting than she could have imagined. She decided to put together all the money she had quietly saved, and think about taking herself away for a holiday. At last she brought the piggy bank out from under the tablecloths where it had been for the last ten years.

Lucy found the hammer, put a tea towel over the piggy bank and stood it on the draining board. Then she gave it an almighty whack and it shattered. She carefully separated the coins from the plaster fragments and dumped the broken pieces into the rubbish bin. Then, scooping up all the money, she carried it to the kitchen table and sorted it into piles. There were lots of five and ten cent pieces, quite a few dollar and two-dollar coins and even some five-dollar notes.

Then with everything sorted, she looked at the one coin left. It was a silver threepenny piece. That must have been what was already in the piggy bank, she thought. Lucy turned it over in her hand, trying to see the date. But it was too small. So she put it on one side and bundled up the rest of the money. There was nearly a hundred dollars and she smiled to herself. She put the silver coin in a separate compartment in her purse.

Next Saturday, Lucy went to the weekend market. The stalls were set out in the back of the car park behind the cinema. You could get everything there – fresh produce, clothes, plants, all sorts of things – and Lucy liked to wander around looking for bargains. She especially liked the antiques. How nice it would be, she thought, to have a little antique shop. New stalls came and went all the time but some of the original holders had been there for years, like the man on the antique and bric-a-brac stall.

Lucy had to settle her mind about something. It was quite a while since she last visited the market and she hoped that the man who ran the antique stall was still there.

He was. Sitting at the back looking just the same as he had for years. He never badgers the customers, Lucy thought. He just sits there reading his book and waits for people to talk to him first.

'Hi,' Lucy said with a smile. 'How are you today?'

Tom Barker lowered his book and stood up to greet her with the shy sort of grin he always had. Blue eyes twinkling under bushy grey eyebrows. 'I'm fine, thanks,' he said. 'How are you?'

'Well, thanks, um...' Lucy was feeling a little foolish. 'I was wondering...' she said. She fumbled in her purse and brought out the silver threepenny piece. 'I don't suppose you remember. But about ten years ago I bought a pink plaster piggy bank from you... Oh, this is so silly, you probably don't remember, it's so long ago. The thing is, you see, I didn't actually break it open until just the other day. And this was in it. It must have been in it when I bought the piggy bank. It's been there all this time. So I wondered if you knew how it got to be in there. It was one of those you couldn't open,' she added, holding out the coin.

Tom wasn't looking at the coin. He was looking at her. 'Yes, I remember,' he said.

'You do?' Lucy was slightly flabbergasted. 'How could you remember after all this time?'

'Because I put it in there,' he said.

Lucy was slightly lost for words. 'You did?' she gaped at him. 'Why?'

'You know, you're the first one who's ever come back to ask,' he said.

'The first one. You mean you'd done this before?'

'Yes,' he stopped, as though embarrassed to continue.

'Well, go on,' Lucy urged.

'OK, well,' he continued, 'when my wife died, I found all these threepenny pieces she'd been saving. She used to put them in the Christmas pudding and that. Well, they weren't any good then – to spend, I mean – because they changed all the currency. So I thought if I put one in a new money box now and again, then maybe it would bring good luck to somebody. Yours was the last one, that's why I remember it. And I thought you looked as though you could use some good luck,' he added.

Lucy shook her head slightly and smiled. 'Well, it's taken ten years,' she said, 'but maybe my luck's changing at last. I'm going to hang on to this,' and she tucked the threepenny piece back into her purse. 'And thank you…er…' she looked at him. 'I don't even know your name.'

'Tom,' he said holding out his hand. 'Tom Barker.'

'Lucy Paget,' she said, noting the firm warm grip, and flushed a little. 'Well, I'll probably see you here again some time,' she managed. 'I'd best be getting on. It must be nearly closing time.'

Tom looked at his watch. 'Yes, I'll be packing up now.' He looked at the floor and seemed to make his mind up about something. He nodded slightly as though to himself. Then he swallowed nervously, and said, 'Would you like to come for a coffee afterwards? I won't be but a minute. Or maybe a bite to eat? I have to call at the shop first, though.'

'The shop?' Lucy asked.

'Oh yes. I have an antique shop on the other side of town. I only come here on the weekends for something to do.'

Lucy felt for the threepenny piece in her purse. 'Thank you, Tom,' she said. 'I think I'd like that.'

Senior Moments

Dusk approached and the elderly lady waiting at the railway station looked anxious. She studied her watch for the third time in two minutes and stretched forward, craning her neck to the right, in the direction the train should be coming.

Nobody else is here, she thought. That's strange. Perhaps the train has gone. But I couldn't have missed it, she decided. I was here nearly twenty minutes early. Something must have happened to delay the train, she thought now. Maybe there has been an accident. She started feeling cross. I'm going to be late, darn it. She looked around. There was a bench nearby. She might as well sit down and rest her legs.

She felt rather alone, and wondered again why no one else was here. The station was completely deserted. She had spent a good part of the day getting ready for dinner in town. Her friend Jess was meeting her at the station and then they were going to that really nice new restaurant. She searched for the mobile phone in the bottom of her bag. She'd better ring Jess to tell her she would be late. She switched it on. Nothing happened. The phone was dead and she remembered she had forgotten to put it on the charger. She was always forgetting to do that. She didn't use it very often and then, when she needed it, it didn't work. Frustrated, she threw the phone back into her bag and settled back on the bench.

She studied her watch. It was the same time as the last time she looked, twenty minutes past seven. The train had been due at seven o'clock.

She looked at her watch again. The little hand had stopped moving. That's all I need, she thought. Now my watch is broken and I don't even know what time it is. She looked around for the station clock.

There used to be one, she remembered, but there wasn't now, just a bare patch on the wall where it used to be. She decided to see if there was anyone in the ticket office to try and find out what was happening so made her way back along the platform to the little kiosk, but there was no one there. She hadn't needed to get a ticket when she arrived; her weekly pass was always tucked safely away in her purse.

It was getting darker now so, making up her mind, she sadly made her way to the side gate which led onto the little parking space where, thankfully, her car was still parked.

It was quite dark by the time Fran arrived home and she wearily put the kettle on to make a cup of tea. I'd better ring Jess, she thought, as she reached into the fridge for the milk. She glanced at the calendar on the door and read her note with the reminder about her dinner date. She checked the day. Yes, Monday. They had decided on Monday because the local train didn't run after six o'clock on Sundays…

The Boardwalk

The boardwalk stretched way into the distance and disappeared into the murky gloom of the mangroves, which towered over the path of wooden boards. It was said to be a delightful walk. It was just over a kilometre long, in a circular direction, and looked harmless enough, I thought, as I made my way through the information centre and out the door at the back through to the entrance of the mangrove trail. There had been nobody manning the reception desk to collect the entrance fee and, after waiting for a few minutes, I decided that I would carry on through, and pay on the way out. It was, after all, midweek and they probably didn't get as many customers as at the weekends.

As I walked down a pathway leading to the entrance of the trail, I found myself feeling a little apprehensive for no apparent reason and gave myself a mental shake. This is ridiculous, I thought. There is nothing to be afraid of. It's just a twenty-minute walk. I had about an hour to spare before meeting my friend for lunch at the pub. I didn't want to wait in the pub by myself, so had decided to do what I had been meaning to do for ages: a walk along the mangrove trail, the entrance to which was only a couple of minutes up the road.

As I went further into the forest of mangroves, it became darker. I was aware that all the outside sounds of people, traffic, everything, had gone.

It was eerily quiet and yet, I thought, not really. I stopped and listened. It was a spooky silence. I could no longer hear the birds. But there were strange squelchy noises and little plops. I leaned over the wooden rails and tried to see what was happening down there in the depths. The tide was out, so the water was very low.

There was thick oozing mud and all the strange-looking mangrove roots were sticking up from the bottom. The low tide was moving the water gently and I thought how the roots looked like fingers of something nasty buried there and gently waving.

Bubbles from some creature under the mud rose to the surface and made a gentle plop as it made a small explosion before falling back into the dark smelly ooze.

It had become cold and I shivered as I made my way further into the mangrove forest and resisted the temptation to turn back. It was also becoming darker. The sun which had shone in bright dappled spots through the mangrove canopy had gone. It was getting cloudy and overcast.

I wished some more people would come along. I felt quite isolated, and my imagination started playing tricks. There was a bend coming up, and I slowed down, trying to walk quietly, half hoping that another human being was around there and at the same time dreading that a scary person was lurking.

Of course there was nothing except the sound of water trickling and those horrible sucking sounds in the mud.

Suddenly I became aware that the water was getting higher and realised the tide was coming in. I remembered reading in the literature that sometimes on a high tide the water came in quite quickly and actually covered the boardwalk.

I started walking faster and skidded on the damp wood. A sliver of fright went through me as I thought, what if I fell and couldn't get up and the tide came in? What if they all went home and nobody knew I was in here? It was all too horrible to contemplate.

Don't be ridiculous, I thought to myself. I can always phone for help. As quickly as the thought came, it passed, as I remembered with horror that I had left my phone on the charger at home.

Resolutely I carried on, walking a little faster, being careful not to slip again. Now and then, I stopped to read the information on boards along the way, about the creatures that lived among the mangroves and the various habitats.

There was another bend coming up and as I rounded the corner I saw a little shelter had been built alongside the path with benches for weary walkers to have a rest.

The next thing I noticed was a leg hanging over the side of the seat. It was attached to a person who was lying full length on the bench and appeared to have fallen asleep. I stopped walking, frozen to the spot. I was quickly aware of thongs, hairy legs, shorts, tattooed arms and a big black beard. I didn't want to disturb him. I didn't like the look of him.

My feet started to move again as I tried to walk very quietly, creeping past the sleeping man. And I was almost past and about level with his head when suddenly he opened his eyes and looked up at me. He must have wondered at my look of absolute horror at that moment as though I quite expected him to jump up and attack me. But he closed his eyes again and murmured something which sounded like 'people disturbing my peace and quiet' and turned over to face the back of the bench.

Feeling somewhat stupid and relieved all at the same time, I carried on walking and after a few minutes saw the light through the mangroves becoming brighter and, thank goodness, the end of the trail as I emerged into daylight again.

It was a short walk back to the entrance, where I paid the young man at the reception desk. I wondered whether to mention the sleeping man, but thought, no, let sleeping blokes lie.

Later, having lunch at the pub. I told my friend I had been around the mangrove trail.

'What's it like?' she asked.

'Excellent,' I said.

Skeleton in the Cupboard

'Look! There's Mad Molly.'

All the local kids called the old lady Mad Molly. She always looked a bit weird clomping around in old boots, with her hair sticking out like she never combed it. She wore layers of clothes which made her look fat and like a bag lady. It was also a known fact that she had lived alone for many years, had never, to anyone's knowledge, had any visitors, or invited anyone in.

She was a regular sight on pension days, wheeling the supermarket trolley containing her shopping down the street to her home, where it stayed on the porch until the next time she shopped. The supermarket people knew about this but did nothing about it. She was harmless, they figured, and the trolley wasn't going anywhere else.

Jimmy and Ben, twin ten-year-olds, were on their way home from school. They had to pass the big old house where the old lady lived and often sneaked a look over the gate as they passed, ready to run if she suddenly appeared. Once when the boys had been standing by the gate, she had waved a stick at them and shouted at them to go away. Today she was unpacking things from her trolley, which was parked by the front door, and taking them inside.

'I bet she's got skeletons in her cupboard,' said Jimmy now. 'Like Miss Baker was talking about at school.'

That day they had been learning about symbolic sayings – when something you said didn't actually mean what it sounded like. 'Still waters run deep' really meant that just because someone didn't say much didn't mean they weren't thinking important thoughts. Having 'a skeleton in the cupboard' meant that someone had a deep dark secret in their past that nobody knew about.

'Yeah, like maybe she was in prison.'

'Yeah, or like she robbed a bank.'

'Nah,' Ben scoffed. 'If she robbed a bank, she'd have a better house.'

Next day on their way to school, the twins stopped again at Mad Molly's gate.

'Hey, look,' Jimmy was pointing. 'The trolley's still got stuff in it. She must have forgotten to unpack or something.'

'That's weird.'

'Yeah.'

'And she hasn't shut the door.'

Indeed, they could see the front door was wide open.

'Yeah,' Ben went still. 'And she never, ever leaves her door open.'

'We better tell Miss Baker.'

'Yeah.'

So they did. Miss Baker, being a responsible citizen, made a phone call, then praised the boys for being observant and doing the right thing by telling her.

That day in class they talked about looking after your neighbours, especially old people. And how it was wrong and rude to give people silly nicknames, and not to judge by appearances.

When Constable Green and Probation Constable Brown got the call out to go and check on Ms Lightbody (which was Mad Molly's real name), they thought it was probably nothing to worry about, just a forgetful old lady. But there was no reply to their knock, so they entered the house, where they discovered old Molly sprawled on the kitchen floor.

An ambulance was despatched and arrived within ten minutes but, as the constables suspected, she had passed away.

'Probably a heart attack,' said the paramedics. 'So sad, being all alone and everything.'

When the boys passed the house on their way home from school that day, there was no sign of the trolley and the door was shut.

'I wonder what happened then,' remarked Jimmy

Their mum told them. 'Ms Lightbody passed away today,' she said.

Excitedly, the boys related their part in the drama, and their mum said she was very impressed by the responsible way that they had acted.

'How come,' asked Jimmy, 'she lived all by herself? Didn't she have any children?'

'No,' said his mum, 'she never married. The rumour was that she had a sweetheart but he went away to war and never came home. I don't know,' she added, 'why she didn't sell that big old house and move to a nice little senior's unit where she would have made some friends, but she always lived alone.'

A couple of days later, everyone found out why she had never sold the house. It was when the second-hand dealer arrived to check out the furniture. They finally found the key to an old store cupboard which had been locked. Inside, there were piles of babies' clothes, stuffed toys, a babies crib and the gruesome discovery of what they thought at first was a doll turned out to be the skeleton of a baby hidden under a pink blanket.

That, of course, made great news for the local papers. The coroner said that the child would have been there for at least fifty years and, as there was no sign of injury, it was probably a cot death. Being an unmarried mother fifty years ago was considered shameful and poor Molly Lightfoot had kept it secret. So sad, everyone said. The supermarket manager started a collection for Molly's funeral because she had nobody left in her family to pay for it.

A local solicitor produced a will made years ago in which Molly had left everything to the Salvation Army. But the furniture was very old and the house so dilapidated it would probably be demolished. All the neighbours turned out for the service in the little local church. They wrapped the baby in a blanket and buried her with her mother.

Next day, Jimmy and Ben stopped by Mad Molly's gate for a moment on their way to school.

'That was totally awesome, wasn't it?' said Jimmy.

'What?'

'Well, you know, Mad Molly actually having a real live skeleton in her cupboard.'

'Yeah.'

'It means, you know, symbolic things can really be real.'

'Yeah.'

Beethoven's Fifth

The attack was over in seconds. Joe lay dazed in the gutter, aware of the pain in his head and the blood on his hands from the gravel where he'd tried to save himself when he landed on the ground. He felt in his back pocket for his phone, but it had gone, as well as his wallet, and he struggled to get to his feet holding his head, aware that it was bleeding. He had been hit with something hard. He looked around to see whether he could see anyone, but the street was deserted. His attacker had quickly disappeared.

It had all happened so quickly. It was dusk and he had been walking home from the station when the man had jumped out from the vacant shop's doorway. He was aware of a hideous Halloween mask and that was about it. Joe leant against the window and looked around for his walking stick, which he had dropped. As soon as he felt a bit steadier, he slowly made his way home, then rang the police on his land line to report the assault and robbery.

They arrived in due course and were sympathetic, but as Joe couldn't give a description of his attacker they didn't hold out much hope for an arrest. It happened too often, they said. Cowardly opportunists targeting the elderly. They told him to try and remember anything at all about the attacker. They offered to take Joe to hospital for a check-up, but he said no, the bleeding had stopped, he just had a lump on his head. There was no real damage done.

Joe cancelled his credit cards and next day bought a new cheap phone. The phone the thief had stolen was Joe's Christmas present from his son. It was the latest model and he was only just beginning to get the hang of it. Joe tried to remember some detail, something that might be a clue. Something that might help the police catch the thug. He thought back. Something was at the back of his mind. And he pictured himself lying on the ground.

Shoes. That was it. He had seen the shoes of the man as he started running away. Blue sneakers with red laces. Joe permitted himself a small grin. Aha!

The next thing was to work out who. Who knew he would be there just at that time? He always caught the six o'clock from the city, where he worked part-time doing the books in his son's shop. It kept him busy since retiring from his office, and he often stopped at the corner deli at the end of his street to pick up milk or bread or a pie, and to chat with Bert the owner. His mind went back to a few nights ago. There was a new man in the back filling the shelves. He supposed Bert had got some extra help. Joe remembered showing Bert his new phone. He also remembered a box of Halloween masks on the counter.

So Joe had an idea. He made a plan. Just to settle his mind if nothing else. He took the next day off, made some phone calls, and the day after called in the shop. Bert wasn't there but the other man was. He took a glance in Joe's direction then quickly walked back behind the counter. But Joe had seen his shoes. Blue sneakers with red laces.

'Where's Bert?' he asked as calmly as he could, though his heart was thumping. He didn't want the man to suspect that he might be recognised.

'He's just stepped out for a bit,' he said. 'Can I help you?'

Joe didn't answer. He got out his replacement phone and dialled his own number. And he wasn't really surprised when he heard the distinct ring tone of Beethoven's Fifth that his son had installed for him. It was coming from the direction of a carry bag on the floor against the back wall.

The man gave a startled glance behind him but didn't make a move. Joe gripped his walking stick. He wanted so badly to use it on the thug's head but common sense prevailed and he turned away.

'I'll catch up with Bert later,' he said calmly as he opened the shop door and let in the two policemen who had been waiting outside trying to restrain an angry Bert, while listening for the opening notes of Beethoven's Fifth Symphony, which were their cue to enter.

Billy Johnson

Billy Johnson had been the lift attendant at the Grand Hotel for twenty years. The Grand liked to uphold its tradition of giving excellent service to its clients and maintained an envied reputation of being the finest hotel in the city.

Billy had a uniform of which he was very proud. Navy jacket and pants with gold buttons and a peaked cap with gold trimmings. He had a stool in the corner of the lift near the floor buttons, the emergency button and the phone. Billy loved his job. He was his own boss, no one told him what to do, he was good at his work and he was well liked by the other staff. He could tell any guest exactly which floor to go to for their room. In fact, he was quite happy with his lot and had no ambition to do anything else.

Billy felt quite important, even when most of the time no one took any notice of him. Indeed, he was largely ignored. Very few people even acknowledged his presence. He was part of the lift mechanism. But he got a little cross (although of course he never showed it) when sometimes a person would lean across him to push the floor button instead of waiting for Billy to say, 'What floor, madam?' or sir, as the case might be. If this happened, he would push the 'stop' button, politely ask which floor they required, and then re-push the button himself.

Billy's shift was from 8 a.m. to 2 p.m. with half an hour for lunch, so he caught most of the people leaving or arriving at the hotel. This was the busiest time in the lift at the Grand. Stopping at every floor all the way up to the tenth and sometimes to the penthouse right at the top, where there was a honeymoon suite for newly weds.

Out of uniform, Billy was a nondescript-looking chap. Small, skinny, going a little bald. His eyes were his best feature. Intelligent bright brown and usually sparkling as though listening to some joke that only he could hear. When at home, he made his meals and watched TV quiz shows and enjoyed pitting his wits against those of the contestants. Billy was also an avid reader, and over the years had become quite knowledgeable. Thus he passed the time and waited for tomorrow to come when he could go to work.

Billy's life was rolling along quite nicely, when one day two of the senior management people took the lift to the sixth floor where the main office complex was located. They were talking about future developments. About how they had to cut down on certain services in order to maintain profits, which apparently had been dropping well below the desired outcome. They glanced towards Billy sitting as usual in his corner with the peak of his hat down over his eyes. He gave the misleading appearance of being completely oblivious to their conversation, but his ears were working overtime as usual. Billy had very good hearing. He heard everything that people were whispering to one another. For some reason people were inclined to whisper in lifts.

'That's one job that isn't really necessary,' he heard one of them whisper, as he quickly glanced towards Billy. 'People should be able to use the lift themselves,' he said. 'It can't be that hard.'

This gave Billy a bit of a jolt. Was he about to lose his job? He finished his shift and went home deep in thought and a tad worried.

Billy had his favourites among the guests There were a few people who lived permanently in the hotel, who did sometimes briefly pass the time of day with him when they used the lift.

One of these was Mrs Graham, a sprightly lady of middle age who had lived there for the past five years. She rarely had anyone accompany her in the lift when Billy was on duty, but always stopped to chat. As she lived on the seventh floor where the permanent residents stayed, she was usually the only one left on the lift when it stopped. One time, she even accepted Billy's help with her parcels to her door when she had a couple of big ones.

Mrs Graham always seemed to be on her own, and Billy thought she must be a bit lonely, but also quite rich, to be able to afford to live in the Grand permanently. He also really liked her. He looked forward to their chats. In fact, now he came to think about it, she always used the lift when he was on duty. Suddenly he realised that if he lost his job, he wouldn't ever see her again.

He desperately needed to know for sure what was going on. So the next time Mrs Graham rode in the lift and there was no one else on board, Billy took the opportunity to ask whether she had heard a rumour about the Grand letting the lift attendants go because of service cuts.

Mrs Graham looked in turn, startled, worried and then very thoughtful as she gazed at Billy for a moment. 'I'll see what I can find out,' she said, then to Billy's delight, touched him gently on his hand. 'You are not to worry,' she added.

Billy's heart gave a little jump as Mrs Graham departed.

A few days later, it was just two o'clock and Billy was about to take the lift down for the last time when Mrs Graham suddenly appeared. He held the door open.

'Thank you, Billy,' she said, 'but I'm not going down just now. I wonder if you could spare a few moments for a chat?'

Billy made a hasty decision, pressed the button for the ground floor and quickly stepped out of the lift before the doors had closed. Mrs Graham turned and beckoned him to follow as she made her way to her apartment. She had left the door open, and to his surprise motioned him to come in.

He had a quick look around. Lots of books, comfy-looking chairs, plants. The TV was on, showing a quiz show. 'Who wrote *Wuthering Heights*?' the host was asking the contestant.

'Emily Bronte,' said Billy without thinking.

Mrs Graham gave him a surprised look. 'Please sit down,' she said indicating an armchair. 'Would you like some tea or coffee perhaps?'

'Tea would be great,' said Billy, still at a loss as to why he was here.

'White with one, thanks,' he added. He took off his cap, for the first time in years conscious of his bald patch, hoping she wouldn't notice.

Mrs Graham moved to the little kitchenette. 'So you like quiz shows?' she asked.

'Um – yes, I watch them a lot.'

'So do I,' she said.

Billy made himself comfortable and watched the show. He answered two more questions and then Mrs Graham brought the tea and some cake, putting it in front of him on the coffee table. She turned the sound down on the TV.

'This looks great, thanks,' said Billy.

'Well,' she said after taking a sip of tea, 'I've had a word with Daddy.'

'Daddy?' Billy was at a loss.

'Yes, he spends most of his time in Europe these days with his new wife, but he still takes an interest in the Grand, and of course still has the final say in most of the important decisions.'

Billy was floundering. 'Um – who's Daddy, then?' he managed.

'My father, Gerard Bertram. He owns this hotel, The Grand. It'll be mine some day,' she added with a twinkly smile. She leaned forward to study Billy's confused face. 'You didn't know?' she asked.

'Well, nobody really talks about Mr Bertram. I thought he was – I – no, I didn't know.' Billy felt so stupid and embarrassed he was at a loss for words.

She laughed, putting him at ease. 'Well, he's in his eighties now, but still as sharp as a tack. He relies on me to let him know how things are going. So I rang him last evening and we had a chat. He's coming back next week for a visit. So those chaps on the board of management will have some talking to do.'

To say Billy was flabbergasted was putting it mildly.

'Anyway,' she said, 'I mentioned the possibility of cutbacks. You know, Billy,' she continued, 'that the Grand has a reputation and tradition for old-fashioned values and service which makes it such a unique hotel. Lift attendants are part of that tradition. There is no way in the world Daddy will let anything change or lower standards. If they want more profits, it will have to come from the guests. Or somewhere else. So you see, you needn't worry. Your job is safe for as long as you want it.'

Mrs Graham leaned back in her chair. She turned the sound back up on the TV. 'It looks as though that chap is about to win a lot of money.'

'What was the name of the TV series starring the Fonz?' asked the host.

'*Happy Days,*' they both chorused along with the contestant.

Billy looked at Mrs Graham, who was looking at him. They both laughed.

'More tea?' she asked.

Billy nodded his thanks and happily settled back in the armchair. This was indeed a happy day.

Keep Off the Grass

It was one of those afternoon tea charity fund-raiser functions, and the home help agency had sent Mary for a couple of hours' work. They were gathered at the luxurious home of Mrs Angela Hopgood, who was renowned for her extravagant tea parties and fund-raising abilities. Mary was slightly awestruck at all the opulence and full of admiration for the beautiful woman who worked so hard for various charities.

Mary was kept busy serving afternoon tea, cake and various exotic-looking pastries.

Back in the kitchen during a lull in the proceedings, Mary had started cleaning up and saw that someone had sent their plate back with the cake almost untouched. So she sneaked a piece to try. It was absolutely delicious. Mary liked to bake, so she decided that after the dishes were done and she had finished work, she would ask Mrs Hopgood for the recipe.

The guests were all having a happy time, cheques were being written, and all of the cakes and pastries were disappearing at an amazing rate.

Mary thought they'd never go. Her two hours' work had passed and it looked like she would be there for another hour at least, which she didn't mind at all. She had really enjoyed mixing with the rich and famous for a change.

Finally the function was over, the guests had gone, the dishes done, and Mary plucked up courage and asked her question.

'Mrs Hopgood,' she said respectfully, 'I was wondering if you would mind giving me the recipe for your lovely cake.'

The lady in question looked askance at the hired help having the temerity to ask such a question. 'Certainly not,' she said. 'I couldn't possibly give you the recipe. It is very special, and handed down by my mother and grandmother. And,' she continued, 'I think it is time for you to go. Thank you for your help. I will contact the agency regarding the hours worked today,' and she rather quickly ushered Mary out the door.

So Mary went home feeling a little downcast but unaccountably happy at the same time.

Next week, she went to visit her brother who had a small farm about fifty kilometres north of the city. As she stopped to unlock the gate at the end of the long track leading up to the farm, a car slowed to pass along behind her and Mary turned in surprise. It was, she was sure, Mrs Hopgood in her distinctive silver Mercedes. She watched the car as it went further up the road and then turned left, disappearing along a track.

Mary was intrigued. So she asked brother Tom, 'Who lives further up on the left? The road doesn't turn there. It looks like a track leading to somewhere.'

Tom looked wary. 'Why d'you want to know?'

'Because I just saw someone I know turn in there.'

'Well, Mary, be careful of this person,' he said. 'They're probably up to no good.'

This was getting interesting, Mary thought. 'Why?' she asked

'Because, sister dear, the only property along that track is another farm, and they grow grass.'

'Grass?' Mary asked, puzzled.

'You know, the kind you smoke. Only it's a bit hush hush. So far the law hasn't caught up with them. All the locals know, but you know the Aussie way – never dob.'

Mary was busy putting two and two together. 'What would happen if you baked it in a cake?' she asked.

'Mary!' Tom was aghast. 'Just don't try it, OK? It could make you happy, or it could make you very sick.' He gave her a quick hug. 'Just you keep off the grass. OK?'

'OK,' she said.

Mary kept the secret and she never dobbed. But her admiration for Angela Hopwood was somewhat diminished and she asked the agency to never send her to that particular residence again.

After all, Mary had her principles.

Green

It was a small unobtrusive house in the middle of an unpretentious street. The homes on either side of the road were all similar. Roofs, doors, windows, all in various shades of grey with pale red bricks. And boringly neat gardens with a little patch of lawn surrounded by shrubs.

When Bobby Joe and Betty May bought their house, they were very happy with the nice neighbourhood, the close vicinity of shops and public transport. There was even a school close by in case they might need it later on. However, Betty May was unhappy. Every time she came home after shopping or wherever, she couldn't help noticing the awful sameness of all the houses. She wanted their home to stand out from the rest, so that when their friends came to visit they could find the house without any trouble.

She liked green. Actually she was a tad obsessed with green. In fact, all the curtains, lounge covers, cushions and so on throughout the house were all in different shades of green. Even the bed linen was green.

Betty May decided to paint the front door. 'A nice bright green,' she said to her husband.

Bobby wasn't particularly fussed. 'Whatever makes you happy, pet,' he said.

So next day Betty lost no time in going to the hardware shop. She looked at all the different shades of green. Sage green, olive green, leaf green, heritage green. She nearly settled for that one, but then she spied the emerald green. That is beautiful, she thought, and exactly right.

'There you go, pet,' she said to Bobby Joe later, 'perhaps you could paint it on the weekend.'

Her husband looked a bit doubtfully at the bright green on the paint tin. 'Are you sure, pet?' he asked. 'It's going to stand out a bit.'

'That's the idea,' said Betty May happily. 'We don't have to be the same as everyone else any more. Now everyone can find us, even at night. You could fix a light over the porch as well.'

So a couple of weeks later, the door was nicely painted. The house and garden were ready for visitors. Lots of green things had been planted in the front, and the greenhouse out the back was full of green stuff growing nicely.

Bobby Joe and Betty May decided it was time to have a house-warming party. They sent invitations to all their friends and family, on which she wrote, 'Look for the house with the green door.'

Meanwhile, the neighbours had been gathering discreetly at one another's homes and making phone calls.

'Have you seen that awful green door?' they said. 'It lowers the tone of our street.'

'This is a very select neighbourhood. It shouldn't be allowed,' they grumbled.

'Well, what can we do about it?' they complained to one another.

They fussed and fumed, had meetings and eventually decided to write a letter to council saying it disturbed the ambience in their neighbourhood to have such an obnoxious-coloured door in their street. Indeed, some people were getting so stressed it was affecting their health and they had to seek counselling. In fact, the harmony of this select neighbourhood was sadly out of tune.

Betty May and Bobby Joe were unaware of the disquiet they were causing and went ahead with their party arrangements for the following Saturday night.

The neighbours watched in amazement as car after car cruised around the neighbourhood, stopping to let people off in front of the green door and then parking further along the street. Some of them came back after twenty minutes or so to pick people up again.

It was a fairly quiet party even though people were coming and going until well past midnight and it all seemed to be very strange, especially to the neighbour Tom Smart, who lived directly opposite, across the road. 'I wonder what's going on behind that green door,' he thought.

After watching from his darkened front room for a while, he had an idea, He unpacked his new camera with the movie app which he had hardly used, and started taking pictures. It was beginning to get dark and some of the pictures weren't too clear until the porch light in front of the green door came on, and then he was getting good shots of all the activity.

Next day, he downloaded everything onto his computer and burned it all onto a DVD. Then he called people from up and down the street. Some he phoned, others he door-knocked.

That night they gathered in Tom's lounge and watched the film in silence.

'That's all well and good,' they said, 'but it's not going to get rid of that disgusting green door, is it?'

'It's evidence,' said Tom. 'Something's strange about that house. I just know it.'

The next night, he was having dinner with his daughter and son-in-law, who happened to be the local policeman. Tom took the DVD with him and explained to his family about what he had done.

'I can't believe you took pictures of all these people without them knowing,' remarked his daughter. 'Isn't that illegal?' She turned to her husband Jack, who had put a stern look on his usually very agreeable face.

'Well, actually, it isn't, so long as you got their permission.' He looked at his father-in-law. 'But you didn't, did you?'

Tom shook his head. 'No, but I think there is something funny going on.' He put the DVD into the machine and switched it on. 'Just have a look. OK?'

Very reluctantly, shaking his head, Jack sat back and watched. He suddenly sat forward. 'Just a minute.' He grabbed the remote control and stopped the video. Then started rewinding back and forth, finally stopping again. He pointed to a figure of a man standing sideways right under the porch light. 'That chap, there. Do you know him?'

Tom shook his head. 'No, I don't know any of them. Why? Who is he?'

Jack was sounding a bit excited. 'I'm pretty sure it's Jimmy Green. He's a known drug dealer. Now, I wonder what he's up to. Since he got out of jail the last time, he's dropped out of sight.' He turned to Tom. 'I'm going to hang on to this for a bit.' He put the DVD back into its case. 'I think you may have something interesting here, Dad. In fact, I think there may be a bit of drug dealing going on. Problem is, we can't use this as a reason to search the place. We need some more evidence.'

'Well, about the green door, then?

'What about it?

'It's an abomination. It looks terrible. Anyway, we are already writing to council to get rid of it.'

'Well, good luck with that,' Jack laughed.

Anyway, off went the letter to council who, strangely enough, took it seriously. After all, this was a high-rate-paying area. They wanted to keep their residents happy. Although people had the right to paint whatever colour they wished on their doors, they still had to conform with council rules for homes in certain areas.

One earnest councillor who lived nearby the street in question offered to hand deliver a letter, which requested very politely that the door be repainted in a neutral colour to conform with council guidelines.

Unfortunately, nobody answered the door, and the councilman, called Derek, thought that maybe the owners were out back. So he headed through the side gate and through to the backyard. No one appeared to be around, and he was about to go back and leave the letter in the mailbox, when the big greenhouse at the rear of the property caught his eye. Being a keen gardener, he decided to see what was growing in it. Maybe, he thought, they have orchids, or tomatoes. He decided that having a quick look wouldn't do any harm.

What he found in the greenhouse made him turn round and scurry away as quickly as possible.

When Betty May came home from shopping that day, she was a little perturbed to find a police car waiting outside the house. Jack had been very happy to get the call from council asking him to investigate. He hoped that this might be the hard evidence that he needed. Indeed, this turned out to be so.

Betty May and Bobby Joe had to sell their house to pay for the enormous fine they copped for growing illegal substances and, as they sadly packed up their stuff, the locals were gathering in Tom's front room, discreetly watching the proceedings from across the road. No one had really paid much attention when all the plants were removed. In fact, someone remarked that they wondered which nursery they were taking them to.

Their main concern was the green door. They had to act quickly before someone else bought the house. So that night when all was quiet, with the aid of torches, gentle mutterings and sshs the door was repainted in a nice shade of grey.

And harmony was restored.

About Harry

We always called him Uncle Harry. My dad's brother. Or that's what my little sister and I always thought. He was our favourite uncle, who was always there for us. He babysat when we were little and invented the most wonderful games. He had a big droopy moustache which was ginger like his hair, warm brown eyes and wrinkles around the sides every time he laughed.

He often stayed for tea and then we would play board games afterwards. Mum and Dad were always too busy to organise such things, and we would chorus, 'Please, Uncle Harry, will you play a game with us?' And he nearly always did. In retrospect, I suspect he let us win a lot as well. Mum always said that she was happy to leave us in Uncle Harry's capable hands and he would sometimes take us on picnics and to the playground.

My sister Betty was always a bit on the cheeky side, and when she was about ten she asked Uncle Harry why he didn't have a wife. He went quiet for a minute. I saw a sad look pass across his face, then he gave one of his big smiles and said, 'What do I need another woman in my life for when I already have two gorgeous girls I can spend time with?' This shut Betty up for a bit, but I had a feeling that she had hit on a spot that made Uncle Harry strangely sad.

One day when we came home from school, Mum sat us down and said in an unusually serious voice, 'There's something I need to talk to you girls about. 'It's Uncle Harry.'

'Why?' said Betty, 'What's wrong with him?

I, of course, immediately thought the worst. 'Is he sick?' I wanted to know, already feeling upset and getting ready for bad news like as if had been in an accident or something.

'No, he's not actually sick.' Mum paused, trying to find the right words.

I was intrigued now and waited for what I was sure was going to be something very important.

'He's in hospital. He's having an operation. You won't be seeing him for a few weeks.'

We waited anxiously for what was to come next.

'Uncle Harry had been having medicine for a while now to help him with the change,' she said.

'What change?' I was perplexed. 'Change for what?'

'Uncle Harry is being changed into a lady. The next time you see him he won't be Uncle Harry any more, he'll be Auntie Harriet.'

This news struck us into silence. We couldn't comprehend the overwhelming information just handed to us. How was such a thing possible? How could our beloved Uncle Harry change into a lady? Betty began to cry hysterically, and I went very quiet, trying to fathom it all out.

Mum looked from one to the other of us and said quietly, 'I know this is hard to understand, so I'll try to explain it better.'

So she did, and eventually we took it all in. How Uncle Harry had always preferred girls' things instead of boys' things. How he wasn't really our uncle, he was Dad's long-time school friend, and when Harry's parents had died, he had sort of adopted our family. Mum and Dad had always known about Harry, and had eventually persuaded him to make the change, and to be what he had always wanted to be, a female. Mum told us not to treat him any differently. He was the same good, kind person on the inside, just as he had always been. He would just look different on the outside.

So that's how we now have an Auntie Harriet. When she eventually came to visit again, it was hard to accept at first. The moustache was gone. The ginger hair had been cut and styled, she had small boobs, which she must have been growing for a long time, but we never noticed. In fact, she looked absolutely beautiful, and now we've got used to it, Betty and I love her to death.

She is learning to use make-up and dress like a lady. In fact, it's really great. She looks happy all the time without that sad look that used to come into her eyes sometimes.

Auntie Harriet doesn't spend so much time at our place any more, but that's OK. Now that I'm about to leave school, I don't play board games so much any more either.

Psychic Dilemma

Rosa worked at the fairground. A big notice up in front of her tent said LEARN YOUR FUTURE WITH ROSA – THE FAIR DINKUM PSYCHIC. She had made the notice herself. Rosa wanted to appear to be real Aussie, although her forefathers were definitely of Roman origin judging by her dark brown eyes and dusky complexion. She was also very attractive, as was evident by the number of men who queued up to have their fortunes told. They always left looking happy, probably because they were even more gullible than women and likely to believe anything they were told.

Rosa was very intuitive. Sometimes she even believed in her so-called psychic powers herself, especially when something she said seemed to resonate so profoundly with the customer. But most of it was guesswork and stating the obvious. The young men or women who wanted their fortune told were nearly always looking for romance.

Rosa was also blessed with great powers of observation. She could usually tell by their manner, their attire, the state of their hands (which gave away so much) and what their line of work was. It was easy to tell the difference between say, a carpenter or any tradesman, from an office worker to a gardener, or, in the case of young women especially, a model or a hairdresser. Palm reading was easy, as were the tarot cards.

People are only too happy to believe in positive predictions. Rosa never gave anyone bad news. If she did see or feel anything negative – and sometimes she did – she never let on.

So Rosa was doing quite well for herself and was looking forward to a break. Tomorrow the fairground would be packing up and moving on to the next town.

Her last customer for the day had been waiting impatiently for his turn. He walked into the tent and slapped five dollars on the table. He seemed to be very agitated as he sat down in the chair across from Rosa. He was quite tall, dark, and had a small moustache which he kept fingering, He was also very obviously gay. Obvious to Rosa, that is, who could always tell.

She tried to put him at ease. 'G'day,' she said with a smile, 'and how are you?'

'I'm good. Yes, thank you.' He spoke with a slight Italian accent.

'Would you like a palm reading? Or perhaps you would prefer the tarot cards.'

Rosa already knew what he would do.

He held out his hand. 'I Just need to know…would you tell me…' he stopped, and suddenly withdrew his hand. He half stood up as though he had changed his mind, but Rosa's gentle smile calmed him and he sat down again. 'I just want to know if you can tell me what my future is. I've had a bad time lately and, well, I think I'm a bit depressed.'

Rosa took hold of his hand and stroked the palm with her thumb. 'Let's see, shall we?'

She had studied lifelines and heart lines and so on, but had never really known whether what they indicated was true, or wishful thinking. Or whether there was any scientific basis in palm reading. She liked to think that she mostly got it right.

'What's your name?' she asked him.

'It's Tony. Tony Alibetti,' he said, somewhat impatiently. 'Why do you need to know my name?'

Rosa didn't answer. She peered closely at his palm. The lifeline was very short. The shortest she had ever seen, and the heart line was divided in two.

She had one of her stronger feelings and took a punt. 'You're having problems with a partner, aren't you, Tony?'

He looked startled. 'How did you know that?'

Rosa smiled and continued her study. He had smooth delicate

hands, neat, well trimmed nails. Not a sign of manual labour. 'You work in an office,' she stated, rather than asked.

He nodded. 'I do, and I need to know – if you can tell me – what do I do?'

'About what?' Rosa needed to find out more.

'Well, see, I love my job. I work in advertising, but there's this person…' He stopped and eyed her suspiciously. 'You're supposed to be telling me my future,' he said, 'not me telling you.'

But Rosa had learned enough. She gave no response. She was getting a really bad feeling about this and wanted the young man to leave. But she carried on. 'You have had problems with another man with whom you had an affair. Now you want him out of your life because he cheated on you.' It was all a very basic scenario.

Tony looked at her suspiciously. 'How did you know that? Well, yes, that's it exactly. So are you going to tell me my future? Is this person going to be out of my life? Will I stay in my job?' His tone had taken a sarcastic turn. He was beginning to eye Rosa as though she had secret information into his not-so-auspicious life.

Rosa was torn. This was a dilemma. His palm had told her he would not live a very long life. But was this necessarily so? Was it true foretelling or was this an anomaly? Rosa didn't want to send the man away with such a dire prediction. She liked to send people away happy. She had to make a decision.

'So, Tony…' she started.

He leaned forward, intent on what she was about to say.

'I see trouble ahead for you, but you will overcome this. Your life will turn around and you will be very happy and at peace. She leaned back, indicating she had finished.

'Is that it?' he asked. 'Can't you be more specific?'

That's it,' replied Rosa. 'I can't tell you any more. The specifics you will have to work out for yourself.'

Tony Alibetti was frowning in thought when he left, but much less agitated. Rosa worried about him for a few minutes, but then put him out of her mind. She started packing up her things to get ready for the men to come and dismantle her tent. They were to be on their way first thing in the morning.

It was probably just as well that she didn't get to read the next day's paper. Though she probably would never have noticed the small paragraph headed, MAN KILLED IN HIT AND RUN.

Antony Alibetti was killed instantly by a hit and run driver at 7 p.m. last evening. Thanks to a witness who took note of his number plate, the driver was later apprehended by the police. He was a co-worker of the deceased and has not yet been charged.

The Bus Shelter

The old bus shelter had been there for many years. Some of the wooden slats were missing, but the tin back which was affixed to the iron roof was still in one piece. Graffitti had been painted on it, and various names and messages were scratched onto the seat and the walls. It smelt of urine.

A middle-aged gentleman was walking along the pathway leading to the seat. He was holding an umbrella and trying to keep it upright against the rain and the wind which had suddenly sprung up. He appeared to be looking for something, or someone. He glanced up and down the path. Occasionally he stopped, walked a little way into the nearby park, looked around, and then returned and continued his journey.

Suddenly his eyes lit up. He had spotted the bus shelter, which had been hidden by a big tree growing alongside and blocking the view, then he quickened his pace as he hurried towards it. With a great smile and a sigh of happiness, he sat down on the seat, closed up his umbrella and stood it down. He leaned back, closed his eyes and sat quite still as though recollecting. It seemed like a happy memory.

After a few minutes, he stood up again and started examining the side and walls of the bus shelter. He put on some reading glasses and peered intently at all the scratched-on messages and names of people long gone. He muttered to himself, sometimes tut-tutting at some of the rude remarks written there. Then suddenly he stopped still and placed his finger on the wall just above the back of the seat. He gently traced round the shape of a heart with his finger. He looked at the arrow still plain to see, piercing the centre and out the other side. The initials PT were on one end and BB on the other.

'So it's still here, then?'

He turned with a smile as he recognised the voice. A lady of the same vintage as himself was folding her umbrella and preparing to sit down.

'Just a minute,' he said. He gave her a big hug, pulled a large handkerchief out of his raincoat pocket and spread it on the seat. 'How are you?' he asked.

'I'm fine, thanks,' she said looking around. 'It's looking a bit grotty, isn't it? But I suppose you'd expect that after all this time.' She looked up at him. 'How did you know the old shelter would still be here?'

'I didn't,' he said. 'I just hoped. I hoped as well that you would remember. It's been a long year this time. I've been looking forward so much to catching up with you again. I haven't been back here for ages. I suppose after they changed all the bus routes, they decided to leave the shelter here as part of the park.'

He took hold of her hand and turned her towards the back of the seat. He pointed towards the heart. 'There it is, see. PT and BB. Can you believe it was thirty-five years ago, and I broke my pocket knife scratching that on there? Still, it's stood the test of time, hasn't it?'

'As have we, Peter. As have we.' She stood up. 'Look – the rain's stopped. Shall we go for lunch?'

As they left the bus shelter, he gave it one fond backward glance. 'Betty,' he said, 'do you remember that time we were in the bus shelter and we…'

She stopped him by grabbing his arm and giving it a little shake. 'Yes,' she said, 'I remember everything. She gave a little smile. 'I haven't forgotten a thing.'

www.ingramcontent.com/pod-product-compliance
Lightning Source LLC
Chambersburg PA
CBHW020346110726
47898CB00003B/1058